TiLLY's BiG PRoBLeM

An Imprint of Starfish Bay Publishing Pty Ltd
www.starfishbaypublishing.com

TILLY'S BIG PROBLEM

Rose Stanley worked as a Student Support Specialist in a New Zealand primary school for six years and has most recently been an advisor for the Lifewalk Trust, where she trains volunteers working in a similar support role. Her work has involved supporting many children as they have gone through difficult life experiences, including bereavement, family separations, and friendship problems. She has also written a number of articles for the parenting magazine *Tots to Teens*.

Lisa Allen is a New Zealand graphic designer and freelance illustrator. She also paints on commission and teaches art. Lisa has illustrated a number of successful picture books for Duck Creek Press, as well as *Mangrove* and *Anzac Day Parade* for Penguin Books.

Also by Rose Stanley and Lisa Allen

TiLLY'S BiG PROBLEM

BY ROSE STANLEY

iLLUSTRATED BY LiSA ALLEN

Tilly had a problem. It was a big problem.
Something was happening in her life,
and she could feel it weighing her down,
making her shoulders sag and her
body feel tired.

She'd told her best friend Ned about
the problem. Ned was her favorite person
in the whole world, and he always cheered
her up. But this time, even Ned didn't really
know what to do about Tilly's problem.

Even though he made his funniest crazy face,
as soon as she stopped laughing,
Tilly felt the heaviness fall on her again.

"Tilly," said Ned, "I think we need to tell a big person about your problem.
A big person can help when you have a big, huge, enormous problem like this."

"Yeah, but who?" asked Tilly.
Ned was quiet for a minute. "We need to make a list."
"A list of what?" said Tilly.
"A list of big people to help you decide who you should talk to," Ned said.

"Okay," said Tilly, "but we have to keep it top-secret."

The next day, Tilly and Ned
met before school, and
Ned showed Tilly what
gear he'd packed for
their top-secret operation.

"I've got binoculars, a watch, a notebook and pencil, and some lollies for energy," he said.
"Good job, Ned," said Tilly. "Let's get started."

It took Tilly and Ned a whole week to make up their list.
It was a bit tricky at times.

Such as when Ned had to go to the nurse's office because he was
sitting in the woods by the adventure playground,
observing the teacher on duty and got stung by a bee.

But they kept looking, and by Friday the list was finished.

Proposed
School Musical
Schedule

  Salad Days
  Year 6

  H.M.S Pinafore
  Year 4

  Barney : The
  Classic Songs
  Year 1

Mrs Jennifer Abercrombie, 49
  Music Teacher, Opera Lover,
  Compulsive 'Glee' Watcher.
  Favourite Musicals - Cats, Evita, Phantom
  of the Opera, Grease, President of the
  Simon Cowell Fan Club!!!

Tilly had four names on her list:

1. Mrs. Abercrombie, the music teacher.

She never yelled at kids, not even when Candice
ripped up all her sheet music while their
class was learning the recorder.

2. Mr. Batte the caretaker.

He always had time for a little chat, and he would tell Tilly and Ned about how great it was to watch things grow.

Mr J. M. Batte

Age : 64

Ex Royal
Marine

Founding Member and
President of the
Petunia Society

Guerrilla Gardener

Neat Freak

Giant PUMPKIN SEEDS

Grofast Beans

SUPER PEAS

3. Miss Leigh.

Miss Leigh was the grooviest, youngest big person at Tilly's school. She knew all the latest words and wore the coolest clothes.

And . . . she worked in the cafeteria.

Miss Amber Tiffany Leigh.

Age 24

Zumba Teacher, Pilates Instructor.

Loves: Cooking, Travel, Clothes,
Shoes. Makes her own earrings.

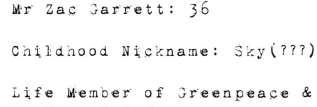

Mr Zac Garrett: 36

Childhood Nickname: Sky(???)

Life Member of Greenpeace &
World Wildlife Fund.

Amateur Ornithologist

Favourite Food:
Ice Cream & Apples
Samosas & Licorice
& Roast Dinners
Place: India
Colour: Orange
Music: Everything
Sport: Golf
Movie Star:
Jennifer Aniston
Book: Lord of the
Rings
Movie: Star Wars
TV: Survivor

 **4.** Mr. Garrett.

Mr. Garrett came to school on
Tuesdays and Fridays, and his job was to
be a friend for the kids to talk to.

"So what now?" said Tilly, after she
finished reading through her list for what
seemed like the hundredth time.

"It's all very well to have a list, Ned, but how
do we decide who I tell my big problem to?"

Ned rolled his eyes at Tilly.
"We make a test, of course!"
"A test?" said Tilly. "What kind of test?"

"It has to be a sneaky test, something that will
show us WITHOUT A DOUBT who is the ONE….
… I'll have to think about it," said Ned.

That's what Tilly liked about Ned.
He thought about a lot of really important stuff that
made Tilly's head spin and her tummy flip-flop.

Although Tilly was getting a bit worried that the
big problem was not going to wait too much
longer, she decided that Ned knew best.

She could be patient!

The next morning when Tilly got to school,
Ned ran up to her and whispered,

"I've got the perfect test!"

"Great work, Ned!" said Tilly. "Let's do it!"
and they ran off together to make
a top-secret and very sneaky plan.

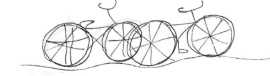

"So, are you ready?"
asked Ned the next day as
they rode their bikes to school.
"I think… I guess… well, yes I am, but
I'm a bit nervous, Ned," said Tilly.
"Be brave, Tilly!" said Ned.

Tilly breathed in a humungous
breath, held it for thirty seconds
and then blew out through her
mouth straight into Ned's face.

"Did you have eggs for breakfast again?" he said, and pretended to have a coughing fit, which made Tilly giggle.

At lunchtime that day, all four of the big people
on Tilly's list received an anonymous letter
in their mailbox. The letter said:

Dear Big Person,

We need some help with a big problem.
Please ~~fight~~ write back to us and tell us why
we should talk to you about it.
Thank you very much.

P.S. Sorry we can't write our names on this letter,
but we'll let you know who we are if you are
the lucky one chosen!

If you're not, thanks anyway!

P.P.S. Please post the letter to this address:
10 Arrow Road, Bethany.

Over the next few days, Tilly got a reply
to each one of her letters.

Dear 'whoever'

I don't know who you are, but I do know that a FREE chocolate covered doughnut cheers up just about anyone! I'll save one for you tomorrow – just come and see me at the tuck-shop.

Luv Miss Leigh

x o x o x

Dear children,

I think that everyone needs to get their fingers into the dirt and remember that problems are like seeds – If you don't feed them, they won't grow!

Please feel free to come and see me if you would like to plant some flowers. Maybe beside the adventure playground?

Mr J.M. Batte

Dear occupant of Arrow Road,

I sincerely believe that if you choose to tell your problem to me, we can put together a lovely song that will help you to express how you are feeling. I look forward to making beautiful music together!

Kind regards
Mrs Abercrombie

Dear person with the 'BIG' problem,
Thank you for being brave enough to ask for help. I would love to talk to you and maybe together we can work out a great plan to solve this problem of yours.
But be prepared — it may take some time!
From Mr Garrett

Once Ned had explained to Tilly what all the tough
words like 'occupant' and 'sincerely' meant,
they chatted together about who would
be the best choice.

"It will be hard to pass up the chocolate doughnut,
but I just don't think Miss Leigh gets it!" said Tilly.
"And I'm not sure that you're really up to making
beautiful music with your recorder just yet,"
said Ned seriously.

"And then there's Mr Batte's letter," said Tilly.
"I mean, how many flowers would I
have to plant to get rid of the big problem?"

"Mmm, true," said Ned, nodding his head.
"So I think you have decided..."
"Yes! I have," said Tilly, grinning.

Tilly started talking to Mr. Garrett
every Tuesday and Friday.
They didn't find a magic solution for her big problem,
but just getting it off her chest helped a lot,
and Tilly knew that in time, they would
definitely work it out together.

Her shoulders were feeling a little lighter each day.

THE END